Ice Crea

Written by Sue Graves

Illustrated by Pete Smith

Contents

 Collins

Questions, questions!

The last question is easy to answer.
We eat ice cream because we like it!

What is ice cream made from?

Ice cream is made from milk **products** – milk, cream, yoghurt or custard – and sugar. Then flavours like strawberry, chocolate or vanilla are mixed in. Special **ingredients** are added to keep the ice cream fresh and easy to serve. Then it is frozen.

Other ices like ice-lollies and sorbets do not use milk products – they are made from water, sugar and flavourings.

The first ice creams

In China

The first ice cream was made in China more than three thousand years ago. It was made by mixing ice with milk and sugar. Making ice cream was a good way of keeping milk fresh.

In Roman times

Then, fifteen hundred years later, the Romans made **water ices**. People say that the Roman **emperor**, Nero, sent servants to run up the mountains to get snow and ice. These were mixed with fruit juices and honey to make water ices.

Marco Polo's ice-cream secret

Marco Polo was a **merchant** from Venice in Italy. He travelled across China for four years, between 1271 and 1275, and some say *he* discovered the secret of ice cream. He then took this secret back to Italy.

Emperor Akbar's ice

Akbar the Great was a Mogul emperor of India in the 1500s. A traveller gave him some ice with fruit juices sprinkled on it. Stories say that Akbar loved this so much, he asked for it every morning. Big blocks of ice were carted across the land, from Kashmir to Delhi. It was a long way and by the time the ice reached Delhi it had melted to a little cupful.

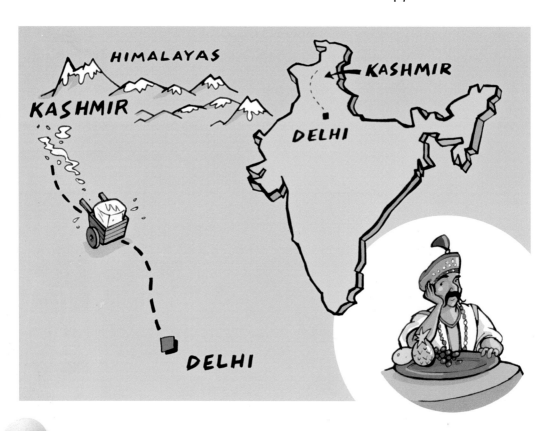

A royal treat

From Italy, the secret of ice cream spread to France and then to England. Not everyone could enjoy ice cream. Ice cream was a **luxury** for rich people only.

Ice cream was first served in England at a **banquet** held by King Charles II in 1672. He didn't want to share ice cream with many people, so only those sitting at his table could enjoy it.

Ice

Until freezers were invented, ice was needed to make ice cream. In winter, ice was cut from ponds, rivers, canals and lakes. It was then kept in underground ice **stores**.

As ice cream became more popular, more ice was needed. Soon there wasn't enough ice left for this in England, so in the 1820s it was **imported** from Norway. The ice was brought to Britain in big ships and stored in specially-built ice wells.

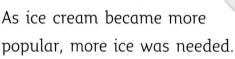

Some large country houses had icehouses in their gardens to store the ice.

Along came the freezer ...

At first, ice cream was mixed in a bowl or a bucket, and it had to be eaten as soon as it was made.

In 1843 an American woman, Mrs Nancy Johnson, invented the **hand-cranked** freezer. Now ice cream could be made much more quickly. By turning a handle, the ice-cream mixture could spin round until it became frozen.

How the hand-cranked freezer worked

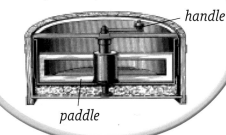

*The handle turns the paddle.
The paddle spins the mixture.*

handle

paddle

TINGLEY'S PATENT
HORIZONTAL
ICE-CREAM FREEZER
Is recommended for FAMILIES, HOTELS, SALOONS, and WHOLESALE MANUFURERS

As the best Ice-Cream Freezer in the market.

It saves ICE,
Saves TIME,
Saves LABOR,

And produces the finest quality of Cream known to the Art.

Send for Descriptive Catalogue.

**CHAS. G. BLATCHLEY, Manufacturer,
506 COMMERCE STREET,
Philadelphia, Pa.**

UNITED STATES PATENT OFFICE.

NANCY M. JOHNSON, OF PHILADELPHIA, PENNSYLVANIA.

ARTIFICIAL FREEZER.

Specification of Letters Patent No. September 9, 1843; Antedated July 29, 1843.

To all whom it may concern:
Be it known that I, NANCY M. JOHNSON, of the city of Philadelphia and State of Pennsylvania, have invented a new and use-
5 ful Improvement in the Art of Producing Artificial Ices, and that the following is a full and exact description of the machinery for carrying into effect the said improvement.
Instead of causing the freezer or vessel ...
ing the accompanying drawing) which ...
the freezer ... to be ...
20 its handle, which tube thus becomes the up-
... support of the said shaft or axis—the ...

... with the beater when the mate-
... come stiff, the handle on the
... in a groove or cavity H 55
side of the cover which
... wooden tub or box I,
... ezing is conducted.
... ented from turning
is ... ke hold of the two 60
... tub being thus cov-
W ... well as the freezer
T ... nded from the heat
... rson of the operator.
... he shaft of the beater
... into a rounded pivot 65
... sponding cavity in the bot-
... eezer.
... nt confine myself to any particular
... terial in the construction of the freezer or
... beater for lemon, orange and other juices 70
... containing acid which might react slightly
... upon tinned iron, I prefer glass cylinders
... for freezers and hard wood or ivory for the
... wings of my beater, for cream and other sub- 75
... ich are not acid in their prop-... is the most

Soon other people started making hand-cranked freezers.

Mrs Johnson announces her new invention.

11

In 1923, a freezer that *kept* ice cream frozen was invented, and that's when the ice-cream **industry** really started. Soon there were **factories** making ice cream and more people could enjoy it whenever they wanted.

Ice cream at the seaside in the 1920s.

Stop me and buy one

In the early 20th century, ice cream was no longer just a treat for the rich. It was sold in cafés and restaurants. Ice-cream sellers sold "licks" – a taste of ice cream on glass. The glass was wiped clean after each lick and then reused. Not very healthy!

In 1923, the first ice-cream bicycles were used in London. Some bicycles had a slogan on the front which said, "Stop Me and Buy One".

The ice creams were kept cold in the metal box at the front.

WAFER BISCUITS 1

STOP ME
AND
BUY ONE

20 T. WALL & SONS LTD
THE FRIARY, ACTON.

WALL'S ICE CREAM

PURE DAIRY PRODUCTS
FRESH FRUIT JUICES
SOUND FOOD VALUE

LARGE BRICKS 1'6
SMALL BRICKS 9ᴰ
TUBS   4ᴰ
CHOC BARS   3ᴰ
BRICKETTES 2ᴰ
SNOFRUTES   1ᴰ

Now you can buy ice cream
everywhere – supermarkets,
ice-cream vans, in the cinema,
leisure centres, at the zoo, the funfair
and on the beach ... where do *you* buy
your ice cream?

The ice-cream cone

There are two stories about who invented the ice-cream cone.
No one really knows which one is true. In England, in 1888,
a cookery writer, Mrs Agnes Marshall, wrote a **recipe** for "cornets
with cream".

Later, in America, at the St Louis World Fair in 1904, an ice-cream seller was selling ice cream on little dishes. Soon all the dishes had gone. Next to the ice-cream seller was a man making **zalabi** pastries from the Middle East. Warm zalabi were rolled into cone shapes and left to cool. Then the ice-cream seller put ice cream into the zalabi.

Which story do *you* think was true?

The I-Scream-Bar

In 1920, in America, a child went into a shop but couldn't decide whether to buy an ice cream or a chocolate bar.

So the shop owner came up with the idea of making a chocolate-covered ice-cream bar. He called it the "I-Scream-Bar".

The first ice cream on a stick was also made in 1920. It was called the **Good Humor** Bar.

What a job!

Today, ice-cream companies pay tasters to eat ice cream.
The tasters make sure the ice cream tastes good and that it has
been made properly. But how can they tell if an ice cream
has a good flavour?

This one's too sweet.

This one's too sour.

When you eat, your taste buds send messages to your brain. Then you can tell if you're eating something that is sweet, sour or bitter. Ice-cream tasters must look after their taste buds!

Crazy about ice cream

- In South Africa, a man ate ten litres of ice cream for charity in under three hours. He said it made his stomach very cold!

- Did you know that there's an ice cream that can burn your mouth? It's chilli-flavoured ice cream.

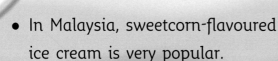

- In Malaysia, sweetcorn-flavoured ice cream is very popular.

- America makes more ice cream than any other country in the world.

- In England, there's a restaurant that serves bacon-and-egg flavoured ice cream.

- People in New Zealand eat more ice cream per person than in any other country in the world.

- Have you ever tried these ice creams – Peppermint Cow, Egg Nog, Rainforest Crunch, Holy Cannoli, Fudge Behaving Badly or Strawberries'n'Cream? Can you think up a new name for an ice cream?

Glossary

banquet	a big feast or meal
emperor	a ruler, like a king
factories	buildings where goods are made
flavour	the mixed smell and taste of something
good humor	good mood – 'humor' is the American spelling of 'humour'
hand-cranked	turned using a handle
import	to bring goods into a country
industry	an organisation that makes things
ingredients	the different things you need to make food
luxury	something that gives you great comfort but which you don't really need
merchant	a person who buys and sells goods
products	goods that have been made – often in a factory
recipe	a list of ingredients and instructions for making something
stores	places to keep things
water ices	ices made with water and not milk products
zalabi	waffle-like pastries from the Middle East

Index

Ideas for guided reading

Learning objectives: referring to text to explain meaning; posing questions in writing prior to reading non-fiction to find answers; using contents and index to find their way around the text; using language and gesture to support the use of models/diagrams/displays when explaining.

Curriculum links: Citizenship: Living in a diverse world; Geography: Where in the world is Barnaby Bear?; History: Why do we remember great people?

Interest words: yoghurt, emperor, luxury, special, restaurant, merchant, leisure centres, charity, Malaysia

Word count: 1057

Resources: card, whiteboard and pens

Getting started

This book may be read over two sessions.

- Explain to the children that they are going to learn about ice cream. Show them the book *Ice Cream!* and read the blurb and contents page (p1) together.
- Ask the children what they know about ice cream. Use this information and the contents page to generate questions about ice cream. Question words (*who, what* etc.) on cards will help. Scribe their questions on a whiteboard.
- Model answering one of the children's questions using the contents and index to retrieve information. Ask the children to try with another question.
- Skim through the book, looking at the illustrations and headings, and discuss what the book is about with the children.

Reading and responding

- Ask the children to read the book silently and independently, and listen to and observe each one reading a short section aloud – prompting and praising for fluency, self-correction and their use of cues to tackle challenging words.
- Ask the children to find out the answers to the questions on the whiteboard using the contents, index and glossary pages. Praise children for using skimming and scanning to find information.